Look Carefully ! And you can find my eyes on each picture.

This is a story about a little unicorn, called Mia.
Mia lived near a river with a waterfall.
A forest of tall trees grew by the river.
Mia and her family were very happy unicorns.
Mia loved asking questions.
"Mommy, what do unicorns like to eat?" asked Mia.
Mommy said, "All sorts of things."

Mia asked another question.
"Mommy, what is all sorts of things?"
Mia's mommy sighed and said she must ask her daddy.
Mia went to ask daddy, but he was resting.
She decided to go and find out for herself.
Mia walked into the forest to find what unicorns eat!

Mia walked along a path and she met a squirrel.
"Hello," said Mia. "What do squirrels eat?"
The squirrel looked up and said:
"Squirrels eat nuts.
Nuts give squirrels big, bushy tails."
"Do unicorns eat nuts and grow bushy tails?" asked Mia.
"Yes," said the squirrel. "Unicorns eat nuts,
but don't need bushy tails.
They have beautiful horns."
"Oh," said Mia and she went along the path.

Mia went deeper into the forest.
She heard a scratching noise on a tree.
It was a bear taking honey from a bee hive.
The bear was licking his sticky claws.
"Lovely honey," said Mia.
"Honey makes bears strong," grunted the bear.
"Do unicorns eat honey?" asked Mia.
"Yes, honey is good for everyone" said the bear.

Mia left the forest and walked by the sea.
She saw a dolphin jumping through the waves.
"Hello dolphin, what are you doing?" asked Mia.
"I am catching fish," said dolphin.
"Fish make dolphins clever.
We eat fish every day."
"Unicorns are clever, do they eat fish?" asked Mia.
The dolphin nodded his head
and Mia went on her way.

Mia sat under a tree on the beach.
It was a berry tree.
Mia heard a loud screech.
She looked up to see a parrot eating berries.
"Hello," said Mia. "what are you eating?"
"Berries, they make me bright and colourful,"
said parrot.
"Do unicorns eat berries?" asked Mia.
"Yeeeees," screeched parrot.

Mia left parrot and his loud screeching.
She walked to a field.
She saw a rabbit eating a carrot.
The rabbit hopped up to Mia.
"Munch, crunch, carrots for lunch," said rabbit.
"Carrots help you see well,"
"Do unicorns eat carrots?" asked Mia.
"Yes, then they see well too,"
then rabbit hopped away.

Mia walked across the field.
She met a cow eating grass.
Mia said, "Hello cow, do you eat grass?"
"Yes! I like grass,
it helps me make milk for the farmer."
"You make milk, how wonderful," said Mia.
"Do unicorns eat grass?" asked Mia.
"Sometimes,
but they don't make milk for the farmer."
The cow went on eating. Mia went on walking.

Mia walked to a garden.
She saw a fat caterpillar.
The caterpillar was eating a leaf.
"What are you eating?" asked Mia.
"Yummy leaf," said caterpillar.
"Green, leafy vegetables are good for you,
They make you grow big and strong,
I will make a cocoon, then I will
change into a beautiful butterfly."
"Can unicorns do that?" asked Mia.
"No," said caterpillar.
"Unicorns don't change, they are beautiful,
but they need to eat healthy vegetables."
Mia smiled and went on walking.

Mia heard children laughing in the garden.
The children were having a party.
It was Jack's birthday.
Jack had a rainbow cake.
Mia knew unicorns love rainbows.
Jack gave Mia some rainbow cake to eat.
Rainbows made her feel happy.
Mia likes rainbows and rainbow cake.

Mia wanted to go home.
She started to cry, then she saw an elephant.
"What's the matter little unicorn?" said elephant.
The elephant lifted Mia up onto his back."
"What have you been doing?" he asked.
"I was looking for things unicorns eat,"
"Oh," said elephant. "What did you find?"
Unicorns eat all sorts of things to grow big and strong,
But I really like rainbow cake," said Mia.
"Rainbow cake is a treat for good unicorns
who eat all their dinner," said elephant.
Mia saw a rainbow shining over the river.
"That's where I live!" she said.
The elephant carried her home.

Mommy was happy to see Mia.
"Mommy, Unicorns eat all sorts of things,"
said Mia.
"and they love rainbow cake!"
"And I love you, little unicorn," said mommy.

Made in the USA
Middletown, DE
20 November 2019